YOU'D BE SURPRISED AT GOD'S PRIORITIES.

GOD WOULD MOVE HEAVEN AND EARTH TO LET ME GO SKIING?

HA!

AND WHY NOT? GOD KNOWS BETTER THAN WE DO WHAT'S REALLY IMPORTANT.

WANNA COME IN?

IS YOUR MOTHER HOME? NO, THANKS!

Matthew 5:43-44

"You have heard that it was said, 'Love your neighbor and hate your enemy.' But I tell you: Love your enemies and pray for those who persecute you..."

New International Version (NIV)

999,969. I will not write "dawgz" in a script ever again.
999,970. I will not write "dawgz" in a script ever again.
999,971. I will not write "dawgz" in a script ever again.
999,972. I will not write "dawgz" in a script ever again.
999,973. I will not write "dawgz" in a script ever again.
999,974. I will not write "dawgz" in a script ever again.
999,975. I will not write "dawgz" in a script ever again.
999,976. I will not write "dawgz" in a script ever again.
999,977. I will not write "dawgz" in a script ever again.
999,978. I will not write "dawgz" in a script ever again.
999,979. I will not write "dawgz" in a script ever again.
999,980. I will not write "dawgz" in a script ever again.
999,981. I will not write "dawgz" in a script ever again.
999,982. I will not write "dawgz" in a script ever again.
999,983. I will not write "dawgz" in a script ever again.
999,984. I will not write "dawgz" in a script ever again.
999,985. I will not write "dawgz" in a script ever again.
999,986. I will not write "dawgz" in a script ever again.
999,987. I will not write "dawgz" in a script ever again.
999,988. I will not write "dawgz" in a script ever again.
999,989. I will not write "dawgz" in a script ever again.
999,990. I will not write "dawgz" in a script ever again.
999,991. I will not write "dawgz" in a script ever again.
999,992. I will not write "dawgz" in a script ever again.
999,993. I will not write "dawgz" in a script ever again.
999,994. I will not write "dawgz" in a script ever again.
999,995. I will not write "dawgz" in a script ever again.
999,996. I will not write "dawgz" in a script ever again.
999,997. I will not write "dawgz" in a script ever again.
999,998. I will not write "dawgz" in a script ever again.
999,999. I will not write "dawgz

Chapter

THERE'S A REASON AND A PURPOSE BEHIND EVERYTHING THE PRAYER CLUB DO
HERE'S WHERE THEY FIND GUIDANCE AND MEANING FOR THEIR LIVES:

"THIS IS THE CONFIDENCE WE HAVE IN APPROACHING
GOD: THAT IF WE ASK ANYTHING ACCORDING TO HIS
WILL, HE HEARS US."

1 John 5:14
(New International Version)

"COME NEAR TO GOD AND HE WILL COME NEAR TO YOU."
James 4:8 (NIV)

"THE LORD WILL WATCH OVER YOUR COMING AND GOING
BOTH NOW AND FOREVERMORE."

Psalm 121:8 (NIV)

 nd Verse

"BUT I TELL YOU WHO HEAR ME: LOVE YOUR ENEMIES, DO GOOD TO THOSE WHO HATE YOU."

Luke 6:27 (NIV)

, AT WHATEVER INT YOU JUDGE E OTHER, YOU E CONDEMNING URSELF, BECAUSE U WHO PASS DGMENT DO THE ME THINGS."

Romans 2:1 (NIV)

"DON'T HAVE ANYTHING TO DO WITH FOOLISH AND STUPID ARGUMENTS, BECAUSE YOU KNOW THEY PRODUCE QUARRELS."

2 Timothy 2:23 (NIV)

BOTTOM LINE:
"DO NOT REPAY EVIL WITH EVIL OR INSULT WITH INSULT, BUT WITH BLESSING, BECAUSE TO THIS YOU WERE CALLED SO THAT YOU MAY INHERIT A BLESSING."

1 Peter 3:9 (NIV)

Join the Buzz!

Move into Serenity's Neighborhood!

Be Part of the Growing Community!

Serenity

Sign up and join at:
www.SerenityBuzz.com

Breaking news! • Contests!
Prizes! • Free stuff!
Answers! • Downloads!
Previews!

Be Part of the Fun and Adventure!

And for more news. information. and projects:

REALBUZZ
STUDIOS

MANGA FROM HEAVEN™
www.RealBuzzStudios.com

SERENITY

ART BY MIN KWON
CREATED BY BUZZ DIXON
ORIGINAL CHARACTER DESIGNS
BY DRIGZ ABROT

SERENITY THROWS A BIG WET SLOPPY ONE OUT TO:
EVERYONE WHO HELPED US GET ON THE CBA BESTSELLER LIST!

LUV U GUYZ !!!

©&T·M 2005 by Realbuzz Studios   ISBN 1-59310-874-5

Published by Barbour Publishing, Inc., P.O. Box 719, Uhrichsville, Ohio 44683
www.barbourbooks.com

"OUR MISSION IS TO PUBLISH AND DISTRIBUTE
INSPIRATIONAL PRODUCTS OFFERING EXCEPTIONAL VALUE
AND BIBLICAL ENCOURAGEMENT TO THE MASSES."

ecpa Member of the
Evangelical Christian
Publishers Association

Scripture quotations marked NIV are taken from
The Holy Bible, New International Version®. NIV®.
Copyright © 1973, 1978, 1984 by International Bible Society.
Used by permission of Zondervan. All rights reserved.

Printed in China.
5 4 3 2 1

VISIT SERENITY AT:
www.Serenitybuzz.com
www.RealbuzzStudios.com